MW01115530

Ready & ABLE Teens:

Ebony's Bad Habit

Ready & ABLE Teens:

Ebony's Bad Habit

Volume 1

A'ndrea J. Wilson

Ready & ABLE Teens: Ebony's Bad Habit. Copyright © 2010, 2012 by A'ndrea J. Wilson. All rights reserved. No part of this book may be used or reproduced by any means without written permission from the author with the exception of brief quotations in printed reviews.

Published by Divine Garden Press
Printed by Createspace
www.divinegardenpress.com

ISBN-13: 978-1453616062

Cover Design: A'ndrea J Wilson
Cover Photograph: ©Kathy Wynn/Dreamstime.com

To the memory of the life and legacy of Sherri Gillis Hailey (1961-2010). We smile as we realized that you are dancing in the streets of Heaven.

September 4th

EBONY PEARSON CLOCKED OUT from her job at Burger World at 8:00 p.m. on the dot. *Thank God*, she thought as she untied her work apron, took off her hair net, and grabbed her purse out of her locker to leave. The night had been a slow one which meant her four hour shift dragged on, feeling more like eight. She enjoyed working and Burger World was a decent job, but periodically flipping burgers and always smelling like old grease was starting to make her reconsider applying for a retail position.

"Alright, y'all. I'm out!" she yelled to her manager and the three employees still working as she walked out of the door.

It was still warm outside, but a small gust of wind let her know autumn was quickly approaching. Tomorrow, school would begin again and summer would be gone like old cassette tapes and rotary telephones. As she walked towards the bus stop, she smiled to herself as she thought about meeting up with her friends from ABLE. ABLE (Adolescent Black Leaders and Entrepreneurs) was an organization designed to encourage teens to become more active in their schools and communities, and to address citywide teenage issues. Ebony had joined the group a year ago and was looking forward to the first meeting of the school year which was being held the next day. She was so caught up in her thoughts about the meeting that she didn't notice the black Honda Civic that had slowed down and was driving next to her.

"Hey Mami," the driver spoke smoothly as he rolled down the window to get her attention.

Ebony, caught off guard, stepped back and peered into the car with suspicion. Recognizing the driver, she laughed, walked up to the car, and said, "Oh, hey

Jaylen! I didn't know who you were. Don't roll up on a sistah like that! I was about to throw the hands."

He grinned and responded, "Nah baby, don't do that. I just saw you walking down the street looking all fine and stuff and, you know, wanted to offer you a ride."

Ebony didn't know what to think. She knew Jaylen Tisdale from around the way and he was cool peoples, but she wasn't sure about getting in the car with him. He must have read the reluctant look on her face because he replied, "I don't bite or nothing. I'm just trying to save you a couple dollars from having to take the RTS home."

She definitely didn't want to take the bus. It would take her over an hour to get home after she took the #24 downtown then transferred to the #6. If Jaylen took her home it would only take about fifteen minutes. "Okay, good looking out," she accepted as she opened the passenger door and slid into the seat.

The ride home was short yet sweet. Jaylen turned on the radio to 104 WDKX which was playing slow jams as a part of their "Quiet Storm" programming.

"Ohhh! This used to be the jam! Turn it up!" Ebony screamed as the intro to Mario's song "Let Me Love You" played. Ebony started to sing and sway her head while Jaylen watched her and laughed. During the ride other oldies but goodies came on including Fantasia's "When I See You," Mary J. Blige's "Be Without You," and Mariah Carey's "We Belong Together." Ebony was having such a good time singing and talking to Jaylen that she was sort of disappointed when she realized that they were already pulling up to her house. As the car stopped near the curb, Ebony unbuckled her seatbelt and reached for the door's latch. "Thank you for the ride, Jaylen. It was fun and you saved me a lot of time."

"Anytime, Babygirl." Jaylen paused and grabbed her free hand then continued, "Listen Ebony. Pardon my forwardness, but I'm really feeling you. So why don't you give me your number and let me holla at you some time."

"Oh, for real?" Ebony asked, surprised by Jaylen's candor. Jaylen responded by nodding his head. Ebony thought about it for a second. Jaylen was cute and he had his own ride, but word around town was that he didn't finish high school and that he was selling drugs now.

"It ain't arithmetic, baby! I'm just asking for your number," Jaylen replied when he didn't get an immediate answer.

"Well . . . okay." Ebony wrote her number down on a random piece of paper in Jaylen's car. "Thanks again," she replied as she passed Jaylen the paper, opened the door and got out.

"Aight, shorty! You be good," he said as he waved goodbye and started to pull away from the curb.

Ebony stood there for a second and watched him drive down the street. She sighed as she considered what she was getting herself involved in. Her friends from ABLE would never approve of her hanging out with Jaylen. However, she kind of liked him and was somewhat curious about what his life was like. *I just gave him my number, I'm not marrying the dude*, she thought as she shook her doubts away and proceeded into the house. On the surface, she wasn't allowing the situation to bother her, but somewhere deep within she knew she should stay far away from Jaylen.

September 5th

THE WEATHER IN ROCHESTER, NEW YORK was always unpredictable and today was no different. Although the day before was warm and sunny with highs in the upper seventies, today was cool and rainy with the temperature around 60 degrees. Ebony had planned to wear a pink halter top, some blue jeans, and her pink sandals, but after a reality check from The Weather Channel, she ended up settling on her black terry cloth sweat suit. The hood from the jacket would help with protecting her recently relaxed hair from the rain.

As Ebony stood in the bathroom mirror trying to bump the ends of her hair with the flat iron, she began to realize just how much she looked like her mother.

Regina Pearson, Ebony's mother, had died a year and a half ago from a short struggle with AIDS. She was a beautiful woman with the same cocoa brown skin and almond shaped eyes that had been passed down to Ebony. Since her mother's death, she and her twelve year old sister, Kayla, had been placed in the custody of her grandmother, Momma Dee. Ebony loved being with Momma Dee, but with her grandmother having diabetes and high cholesterol, Ebony was always worried about who would care for them if Momma Dee passed. Their father lived in California, and with the exception of sending his court ordered monthly child support check of $200, they rarely heard from him.

Money was tight at Ebony's house. Momma Dee received a social security check of $625 and $1000 combined checks from the death of their mother for Ebony and Kayla. After adding the child support monies, the three of them were expected to survive on less than $2,000 a month. After the mortgage, utilities, Momma Dee's medications, and groceries, little to nothing was left. Being sixteen years-old, Ebony took on a part time job to help buy clothes for herself and her sister and to have a bit of spending money.

After her mother died, Ebony had very little time to mourn. She was living in Atlanta, but had to immediately move to upstate New York to live with Momma Dee. For Kayla's sake, Ebony stayed strong and pushed the pain deep down within herself. At times like this, she found herself drifting off into thought about her mother, wishing life had dealt her a better hand. She looked in the mirror again wiping away the tears that were threatening to take over her face and took a deep breath. "Get it together," she ordered herself, refusing to fall apart. "Now is not the time," she said to herself, and in the same breath yelled down the hall, "Kayla, hurry up!"

By the time she finished getting dressed, Momma Dee was in the kitchen cooking grits, toast, eggs, and bacon: a first day of school ritual.

"Morning, Momma Dee," Ebony said as she sat down at the kitchen table, waiting to be served a hot and tasty breakfast.

"Morning child, where's yo' sister? She gonna miss this bus if she don't come on," Momma Dee replied as she stirred the cheese grits to keep them from clumping up.

"I know, I told her! Kalya! Momma Dee said you better come on!" Ebony shouted.

Momma Dee placed two plates on the table for the girls and began washing the dirty pots and pans in the sink. "You gotta work tonight?"

Ebony began eating her food quickly, not wanting to be late herself. "Not tonight, but I got an ABLE meeting after school so I won't be home 'til later."

Momma Dee turned around and faced her, smiling. "That's real good baby. Yo' momma would be so proud to know you was doing so well and hanging with them smart kids."

"Yeah, she would," Ebony replied looking down, not wanting her grandmother to see the sadness in her eyes.

The first day back at school was the same as always: people rocking their newest and flyest gear, heartfelt embraces to people you haven't seen in three months, confusion over incorrect schedules, and scoping out the new students better known as "fresh meat." The day went on pretty much uneventfully until the dismissal bell rang. Ebony was at her locker putting away her science book when her best friend Fawn met up with her. Fawn was also a member of ABLE and the two had planned to ride together to the meeting. Fawn was a spoiled rich girl who, although she only had her license for three months, already had a brand new Acura.

"Hey girl," Fawn sang as she approached Ebony.

"Hey," Ebony looked past Fawn as if she was searching for someone. "Where's your man?"

"Who Ledell? I left that fool with O. He's gonna catch a ride with him." Fawn loved to say the word "fool" so much that, at one point, she was jokingly nicknamed "That Fool." Omar better known as O. was the school's star basketball player and the Vice President of ABLE. The four of them were the only students from Edison High School involved in the group so they usually car pooled to meetings. The other members were from different high schools including School of the Arts, Wilson, Marshall, East, and Franklin.

Fawn searched through her Baby Phat purse for her car keys while Ebony slammed her locker shut and began walking in the direction of the parking lot. "I hope Alisa ain't trippin' today," Ebony said pushing the exit door open and walking out into the gloomy outdoors. Alisa was the president of the group and was known for "getting her panties all in a bunch."

"I know that's right! That girl really needs to chill out," Fawn said as she headed towards her car. She was almost to her driver side door when a car sped up and then slowed down in front of them. "Now, who is this fool?"

Ebony didn't reply. She knew it was Jaylen. He pulled to the side of them and rolled down his window.

"How ya'll ladies doing?" he coolly asked, smiling seductively at Ebony.

Fawn, recognizing him, unlocked her door and nonchalantly replied, "We alright Jaylen. Just got somewhere to be."

Jaylen pretended not to hear her and continued to speak to Ebony. "You real look nice today, but you always look good."

"Oh, thanks." Ebony tried not to blush. By this time Fawn had gotten into the car and turned on the engine to give Jaylen a sign she was ready to go.

Understanding Fawn's hint Jaylen said, "I guess your girl's in a hurry. It's cool though. Just so you know. I plan on using that number tonight." He smiled again and pulled off rolling up his window at the same time.

Ebony got into the car and Fawn was grilling her. "What was that all about?"

"Nothing! He just gave me a ride home last night!" Ebony said defensively.

Fawn turned her body toward Ebony with shock in her eyes. "What? You got in that dude's car? What in the world were you thinking? You know he sells drugs, right?"

Ebony rolled her eyes. "It's not like that. I was just really tired and didn't feel like waiting on the RTS. Everybody ain't got a rich momma and daddy like you that will buy them a car at seventeen! Chill out. It's not even that deep."

Fawn pulled out of the parking lot, shaking her head in disgust. "It better not be 'cause nobody's trying to hear you getting involved with that fool. You got too much going on for yourself to even get wrapped up in his drama."

"I know, I know! Can we drop the subject?" Ebony looked out the window irritated. She knew her friend was right, but she didn't like to be questioned like that. Not only that, but the verdict was still out on Jaylen. His selling drugs was at this point just a rumor. Underneath it all, she found herself excited about her run in with him. And she was looking forward to his phone call despite Fawn's warning.

When Ebony and Fawn walked into the ABLE meeting, Ms. Lena Washington, the organization's advisor, was heading to the podium to start the meeting. The girls quickly took a seat next to Desiree, Latoya, and some girl they had never seen before. *She must be a new recruit*, Ebony thought. Fawn looked around the room, attempting to locate Ledell. Upon spotting him across the room sitting with Omar, Martel, Victor, and Trenton she redirected her focus to the front at Ms. Washington.

"Welcome to the first ABLE meeting of the school year," Ms. Washington began. "We are glad to see that many of you have returned to commit another year to academic excellence and community responsibility. We know with this being the first day back at school you guys are tired so we will not make this a lengthy meeting. I will now turn the podium over to Mr. Tony Armstrong, ABLE's Founder and Chairman."

Loud cheers and applause broke out as Mr. Armstrong approached the podium. "Thank you, thank you," he responded. "I am very excited about the work we will be doing in our schools and communities this year. When I started ABLE six years ago, I only dreamed that I would meet outstanding young people like the group sitting before me.

"The people in this room prove that teenagers can be mature, focused, and successful. There are many others your age who are wasting their lives by being unproductive, misguided, and unprepared for life. True success in life is not about luck or circumstance, but about choices. The members of ABLE are choosing to be positive leaders in their schools and environment. Each one of you is choosing to invest in your future and not be deceived by a world that tells you that you cannot be powerful and influential. You are choosing to walk away from ordinary life to be extraordinary." Cheering and applause began again. "Now that you are feeling empowered, I am going to call to the podium Alisa Grant, this year's ABLE President."

Clapping continued as Alisa moved towards the podium. Alisa was wearing a blue button up dress shirt, black wide leg dress pants, and black peep toe wedges. *That is so Alisa*, Ebony thought shaking her head at

Alisa being seventeen, but wearing thirty-year-old woman apparel.

"Greetings fellow ABLE members. I am honored to serve you as your president this year. Our first order of business is to vote in our newest recruits. We currently have two applicants that have expressed interest in joining the group and have met the qualifications, as well as passed preliminary interviewing. As a reminder, to be considered for membership one must maintain at least a 3.0 Grade Point Average or B average, participate in an extracurricular activity which may include a sport, club, volunteer, part-time employment, or own a business. The final criteria are successful completion of interviewing with the ABLE membership board and sponsorship by a current member.

"Tamia Fisher and Rashan Watson have successfully completed the application process and desire membership in this organization. Will these two please stand and come forward?" The new girl sitting next to Latoya and an unknown boy across the room stood and proceeded to walk to the front of the room.

"Tamia Fisher is a fourteen-year-old freshman from Franklin High. She maintains a 3.2 GPA and her activity is softball. Her sponsor is Latoya Arnold. All in favor of membership for Tamia say 'aye'."

Ayes were heard all over the room.

"All opposed say 'nay.'" Silence.

"The ayes have it. Rashan Watson is a fourteen-year-old freshman from Marshall High. He carries a 3.5 GPA and his activity is volunteer work at a homeless shelter. His sponsor is Martel Douglass. All in favor of membership for Rashan say 'aye'."

Once more ayes were heard around the room.

"All opposed say 'nay.'" Again silence.

"The ayes have it. ABLE members I introduce you to our two newest members, Tamia and Rashan."

Once again applause filled the room. Tamia and Rashan smiled happily as they took their seats.

"Continuing on," Alisa said. "As most of you know, every month we choose a social issue from our project box to work on as a group. I would like to remind you that the box is located in the right hand corner of the room and suggestions can be dropped in the box at any time and by any member using the designated form. This month's project is AIDS and teenagers. Are there any ideas of how we can educate our city on this topic?"

"What about passing out condoms at high schools?" Trenton asked.

"But we have to do more than just passing out condoms. Most kids have condoms, but it's about getting them to use them," Martel responded.

"What we need to do is promote abstinence," Desiree replied.

"True, but we all know teens are not going to stop having sex," Latoya commented.

"Maybe we can stress the benefits of both abstinence and safe sex," Omar said.

Ebony knew firsthand the importance of the subject. She felt excited about the chance to help others avoid the pain she had felt for the past few years. "Well, as most of you know my mother died from AIDS. People don't take this thing seriously until it happens to them or someone they love."

"So do you have any suggestions of what we can do?" Alisa Asked

"I was thinking that maybe we could have a citywide talent show and give the proceeds to AIDS victims in our own city," Ebony answered anxiously.

"That's a great idea!" Ledell replied.

"We can educate people about the disease throughout the show," Fawn added.

"And each ticket we sell we can give that person a red ribbon to wear on the day of the show," Martel said.

Alisa jumped in excitedly. "These are all really good ideas. I say we vote on this project. What should we call it?"

"Let's call it . . . Project: Wise Up," Ebony enthusiastically suggested.

"Perfect! All in favor of 'Project: Wise Up' say 'aye'."

Again ayes filled the room.

It was after seven in the evening when Ebony got home. Momma Dee was in the kitchen frying catfish and her sister Kayla was playing double-dutch down the street with some of her friends. Ebony sat down on her bed thinking about the AIDS project and how much it was a great opportunity for her to share her story with others. She looked at the picture of her mother she had hanging on the wall, pasted on a collage with other pictures of her friends and family and thought, *You'd want me to do this*.

In the middle of her thoughts her cell phone rung, displaying a number she was unfamiliar with.

"Hello," she answered hesitantly.

A deep and masculine voice responded, "What's up, sweetheart. Do you know who this is?"

It had to be him. "Jaylen?"

"Who else would it be? I'm assuming you don't have a man."

"Nah, not right now." After answering she wished she hadn't said it so quickly.

"Cool, 'cause I plan to fill that position."

"Boy stop!" she said giggling at his obvious flirtation.

"I'm for real. But anyway . . . So your girl Fawn don't like me, huh?"

He must have picked up on Fawn's attitude.

"She doesn't know you, but she thinks you're trouble. Are you?"

"A little trouble can be good. But nah, I wouldn't call myself trouble."

She picked up a pen and began doodling on a nearby notebook. "So what would you call yourself?"

"Uh, let's see . . . maybe someone who knows when to take advantage of a good opportunity." He seemed to have an answer for everything.

She stopped writing. "Oh really? So let me ask you something else."

"What's on your mind? You can ask me anything."

"I heard you in the drug game. Is this true?" she asked nervously.

"Baby I'm a business man; I don't have time for games."

"So it's true?" she asked again boldly.

"Listen, forget all that. I called you 'cause I'm really feelin' you. You're cute, got a nice shape, and you seem real smart. I like that in a female. I can tell you diggin' me too. So why don't you forget all that stuff your friends are saying about me and take the time to get to know me yourself. Is that cool?"

He was right. She wanted give him a chance, but she knew her friends were going to "let her have it" about this guy. "Yeah, it's cool." She began doodling again.

There was an awkward silence. Ebony was about to make up an excuse to get off the phone when Jaylen spoke. "So when do I get to spend some real time with you? You know, take you out or somethin'?"

She thought about her schedule for a second then said, "Well I gotta work on Friday, but Saturday I get off at 3:00 p.m."

"That'll work. So I'll come scoop you around 6 o'clock . . . You know, I'm looking forward to making you my girl."

Jaylen was acting like he really wanted to be with her and she couldn't believe it. "For real?"

"For real." Ebony smiled as she pressed the end button on her phone. She thought about Fawn and her warning about Jaylen. *Fawn is not my momma and I just won't tell her*, she thought as she took off her shoes and started to get ready for dinner.

September 6th

THURSDAY SEEMED TO DRAG by as Ebony spent most of her time daydreaming about her upcoming date with Jaylen. After school, she was hanging up flyers on the bulletin boards of various high schools with Fawn, Ledell, and Omar when Fawn caught on that she was acting strange.

Jaylen walked up behind Ebony and wrapped his arms around her waist. Ebony folded her hands around his and pulled him closer. She turned her head to the right and leaned over a bit to make eye contact with him. He looked into her eyes and leaned in to brush his lips against hers . . .

"Ebony! Hello!" Fawn yelled as she waved her hand in front of Ebony's face to bring her out of her daydream.

Ebony winced twice, realizing she had zoned out again. Trying to play it off she said, "Dag, why you got your fingers all in my face?"

"Cause you need to snap out of it. What's been up with you lately? You've been buggin' since Monday."

"I'm alright, just a little tired," Ebony attempted to lie.

"Whatever you say E. You better get your head in the game because this talent show thing was all your idea."

Ebony loved Fawn to death, but she was so annoying. "You don't have to remind me."

Fawn noticed the edginess in Ebony's voice. "What's up with the attitude?"

"I'm cool," Ebony said while taping another flyer to the hallway wall at Wilson High School. Changing the subject quickly she asked, "So did you see the way

Martel was looking at Desiree at the ABLE meeting? That boy got it bad for her!"

Relieved to talk about something else, Fawn responded, "Yeah I peeped that. I don't know why they just don't stop playing and hook up. That whole 'we're best friends' thing is so played out!"

"I think he's down, but you know Desiree. She is so glued to that newspaper I'm surprised she even makes time to eat!"

"Well she better wake up and smell the coffee before someone else takes that. Martel is fine and plenty of chicks like him. Matter-of-fact, I heard that girl Lashay likes him."

"Lashay who?"

"You know that cheerleader from East. The one with the huge booty and the light eyes that all the dudes be breakin' their necks over."

"Oh Shay-Shay? Yeah, I know who you're talking about. She lives a few blocks away from me. She's alright, but personally, I don't think she's all that."

"Me neither, but you know black folks always think you are cute if you got features that are not typically associated with being black. I'm so glad my parents taught me the true beauty of a black woman or I'd be over here losing my mind over not being light enough."

"Right! My mom was big on telling me I was beautiful, too." Ebony began to reminisce about the way her and her mom would look in the mirror together and compliment each other on their smooth skin, dark hair, and gorgeous smiles. She missed that. Her mom always made her feel so lovely and so special. With her mother gone, she now felt lonely and lost.

Fawn could tell from the look on Ebony's face that she was starting to drift off into space. Ebony had always been a little distant, but lately her daydreaming was happening too much. Fawn knew Ebony still struggled with her mom's death. Being best friends, Ebony felt comfortable coming to Fawn with her tears and depression over her mother's passing. Fawn felt responsible for helping Ebony deal with her hurt and not getting caught up in negative coping techniques.

That was why she didn't trust Jaylen hanging around Ebony. He was a bad influence and the last thing Ebony needed right now was someone offering her a pipedream. Jaylen was the type of guy to introduce Ebony to a lot of experiences that could ruin Ebony's life. Fawn didn't think Ebony was dumb, but she knew that Ebony was vulnerable and her vulnerability could lead her into a lot of trouble.

"Earth to Ebony!" Fawn, once again woke Ebony out of her trance.

Ebony blinked and refocused her eyes on Fawn. "What? Uh, what you say?"

"Nothing." Fawn shook her head. "You just started zoning out again. Are you okay?"

Ebony broke eye contact with Fawn and glanced down at the ground. "Yeah. Just thinking about my mom, but I'm alright."

"That's what I thought. I got an idea. Why don't we finish up these last few flyers and go get a pedicure? My treat." Fawn smiled, knowing it was a deal her friend couldn't pass up.

"Ohhh! That sounds nice. I'm definitely down for that."

"I bet it does. All that working at Burger World got your dawgs looking all ashy. And I know I saw a bunion on your big toe!" Fawn joked.

"Yo' momma got a bunion!" Ebony joked back.

Fawn laughed. "Don't get mad cause your feet nasty! Hurry up and post that flyer so I can take your hammertime looking feet to get scraped!"

September 7th

EBONY CHECKED THE ORDER TICKET one last time to make sure all the items were in the bag. *Two bacon, double cheese burgers, one large fry, one order of onion rings, and one chicken sandwich*, she read to herself. She peered into the medium sized, brown paper bag and eyed the items she had just read. Feeling confident that all of the items were accounted for, she grabbed the bag from the steel countertop and walked towards the drive-thru window. Pushing the small, double windows open, she passed the bag to the occupant of the car sitting outside of the window.

"Thanks and have a good day," she replied robotically to the customer before pulling her hand back and closing the double windows.

She glanced hopefully over at the large, white clock on the wall, praying that her shift was nearing its end. *Cool*, she thought. Twenty more minutes and she would be able to go home. Tonight had been a typical Friday evening at Burger World. It had been slow until dinnertime, around 5 o'clock, and then it got super busy and stayed that way until about 8 p.m. It was now 8:40 p.m. and Ebony was starting to feel the fatigue from the long week.

Over the summer she had worked mostly weekdays, but now that school was back in session, she had been scheduled to work mostly weekend shifts. Although she didn't mind working on the weekends, she knew that she would end up missing a lot of social functions because of her work schedule. After holding down a job for a year, she was used to being the party pooper, and often people no longer invited her to events because they knew the response would be the same: She had to work. As much as she hated to forgo the fun, her weekly paychecks were a constant motivation to remain faithful to her job. She loved buying things for her little sister Kayla and being able to pay for school materials without having to ask her grandmother for the money. It made her feel even more proud when she had a little money left over and was able to give her grandmother a few extra dollars for groceries. Momma Dee always tried to turn the money down, but Ebony insisted. She was determined to keep her promise and help out as much as she could.

The drive-thru bell went off, letting Ebony know that another customer was at the speaker, ready to order. Ebony regained her position in front of the register and pressed the button on her ear piece so that she could talk to and hear the customer. "Welcome to Burger World, home of the Universal Burger. Can I take your order?"

"Um, yeah!" the customer screamed.

Ebony hated that. She could hear just fine. They didn't have to scream. "Go ahead with your order, Ma'am."

"Uh, let me, uh . . . Can I get a Whopper?"

Ebony sighed. Another thing she hated was people getting confused and attempting to order things that Burger World didn't offer. "Ma'am, this is Burger World, not Burger King. We don't sell Whoppers here. Would you like anything that is on the menu in front of you," Ebony said feigning politeness.

"Oh, I'm sorry. Dag, y'all don't got Whoppers? Awe man! Well in that case, let me get two #4's. Y'all don't sell milkshakes either?" The irritating customer giggled.

Ebony took a deep breath and repeated to herself, *Only a few more minutes and I'm off. Only a few more minutes and I'm off.* "No we don't sell milkshakes either. All of our beverages are listed at the bottom of the menu."

"Alright, well, let me get two Cherry Colas then."

Ebony keyed in the customer's order on the resister then asked, "Will that be it?"

"Yeah, I guess."

Hitting the total button, Ebony responded, "Your total is $10.79. Please drive around to the second window." She folded her arms and waited patiently for the car to drive around, mentally asking for the strength not to screw-face the annoying customer.

As the car pulled up to the drive-thru window, Ebony burst into laughter. Fawn smiled innocently at her from the car while Kayla sat in the passenger seat, giggling and waving.

"Oh my goodness! I was about to straight go off! Y'all play too much!" Ebony ranted as she leaned out the window to talk to them.

"I knew you were steaming! I would have kept going, but I didn't want to get you fired for letting me have it!" Fawn joked.

"We got you, sis!" Kayla exclaimed.

"Yeah, y'all got me good." Ebony leaned further out of the window. "What are you two doing here anyway?"

Fawn shifted the car into park. "I stopped by your house and Momma Dee said you were working so I figured I would bring Kayla to get something to eat and pick you up from work."

"Awe! That's so sweet! Thanks for looking out for your girl!" Ebony gloated.

"No problem, sweetie!"

Ebony began to pull her body back into the restaurant and glanced back at the ticking white clock. "Well let me get your order and then you can park and wait for me. I get off in ten minutes."

Fawn nodded. "Sounds like a plan. And hey, don't be stingy with the fries!"

Ebony smiled and rolled her eyes at her greedy friend. "Hush!"

September 8th

WHEN EBONY GOT HOME from work on Saturday it was already 4:30 p.m. She took a hot shower, moisturized with baby oil, and ironed her clothes. She decided to wear a pair of blue jeans, a chocolate-colored tube top, and an off-white cotton mini jacket. By the time she was applying her lip gloss and smoothing out her ponytail, her cell phone rang, letting her know that Jaylen was outside waiting. She put her big, gold hoop earrings in her ears, took one last look in the mirror, and headed for the door. Walking to the car, she looked around to make sure no one was watching. She did not want word to get back to her friends that she was out with Jaylen.

"Hey cutie," Jaylen spoke as she slid into the passenger seat.

"Sup Jay. So where we going?"

"I was thinking we could catch a movie. I really want to see that movie about the pimps who go undercover for the FBI . . . you know the one I'm talking about?"

"Yeah, uh . . . "Pimpin' the Po Po", right?"

"Yeah, that's it! Then if it's not too late we can grab something to eat. Are you hungry?"

"I'm okay for now." Ebony smiled at Jaylen and turned her head to look out the window. He seemed so nice and he was really interested in her. Too bad her friends couldn't see this side of him. She felt good about hanging with him, and she wasn't going to let anyone decide for her who she would date.

During the movie, Jaylen was a gentleman. He bought her popcorn and a soda, let her pick the seats, and didn't try anything more than putting his arm around her shoulder. After the movie they went to a restaurant called *Friendly's* for burgers and fries. They talked all night about the movie, their families, her school, and ABLE.

"So y'all help other teenagers?" Jaylen asked, fascinated by her description of ABLE.

Ebony sipped her milkshake and responded, "Yeah, you could say that."

He smiled. "So you must be real smart, huh?"

She blushed. "Not really, I'm a decent student. My friends really get on me if I start slacking, so they help me keep my grades up."

"That's tight. I wish I had true friends that looked out for me like that. But then again, I do. I got you, right?"

Blushing again she replied, "Right."

Jaylen gulped down his soda. "Uh . . . speaking of friends . . . does your girl Fawn know you're out with me tonight?"

"Uh, no. I didn't tell her." Ebony bit her lip unsure of how he would take her response.

He placed his glass down on the table. "Why not? Are you embarrassed of me or somethin'?"

She shook her head quickly. "Naw, Jay. It's not like that."

He reached across the table and grabbed her hand. "So tell me what it's like."

Ebony shrugged. "It's not like nothin'. She don't need to be all in my business."

"I thought she was your best friend."

"She is, but it doesn't mean I have to tell her everything I do. I'll tell her about us when I feel it's necessary." Ebony smiled as he rubbed her hand softly.

"You sure you're not ashamed of me."

"I'm not ashamed."

"Okay. Good." He smiled confidently, released her hand, and took another gulp of his cola.

When Jaylen pulled up to Ebony's house to drop her off it was almost 10 p.m. Ebony unfastened the seatbelt and turned towards him.

"I really had a good time tonight. Thanks for the movies and the food."

"It was my pleasure. So when I'ma see you again?"

She wanted to see him again, but didn't want to risk getting caught by Fawn. Although she told him she wasn't ashamed of him, she really did worry about Fawn's disapproval. "I don't know . . . maybe next weekend?"

He took a deep breath in disappointment. "I don't think I can wait that long. What about I take you to school on Monday?"

Someone would definitely see them together if he took her to school. That was out of the question. "I'm not sure if that's a good idea."

"Why? You scared of what Fawn gonna say?"

"It's not that, it's just–," she began, but was quickly interrupted.

"Look baby, I really like you and honestly, I want you to be my girl. It ain't a problem with me taking my girl to school. You shouldn't have to catch the city bus when your man got a car, you feel me?"

"I feel you." She felt so stupid. He really liked her and she was rejecting him because of other people's opinions.

"So are we going to do this? You gonna be my lady or what?"

Wow, Ebony thought. *This is moving faster than I expected. I'm feeling him, but being committed is a big deal.* "Don't you think it's kind of fast?"

"Not at all." Jaylen sat up and looked at her before asking, "What? You seeing someone else?"

"No."

Jaylen sat back and gestured to say, *what's up?* "Either you like me or you don't, but tell me something."

"I do like you." She leaned back on the seat and sighed heavily. *What should I do?* she thought. *I've hung out with a few guys before, but I've never had a real boyfriend before. It might be nice to have someone in my life. Fawn has Ledell; why shouldn't I have someone too?*

"Okay, why not?" she said, shrugging her shoulders in surrender.

"That's what I'm talking about. Now give your man a kiss right here," he said pointing at his left cheek. She leaned over and pecked him on the cheek, still a little confused about what just happened.

"So I'll see you on Monday morning, but I'ma call you tonight."

"Okay, bye." *How did I get myself into this situation?* she asked herself as she walked up the porch stairs and inserted the key into the lock on the front door. Turning around and watching Jaylen speed down the street she felt happy, uncertain, and worried, all at the same time.

September 9th

SUNDAYS WERE USUALLY RESERVED for
Kayla. Ebony would take her to church in the morning
then spent the afternoon and evenings helping her with
homework, washing and braiding her hair, and taking
her out to the movies or other local events. This
particular Sunday, the local chapter of Zeta Phi Beta
Sorority Inc. was hosting a Family Reunion Barbeque
at Genessee Valley Park to bring all of the local Pan-
Hellenic Greeks together in the spirit of unity. All black
fraternity and sorority members and their friends and
families were invited to the event. Mrs. Simmons,
Kayla's best friend Jasmine's mother, being a member
of the hosting Zeta chapter, invited Kayla and Ebony
and drove the girls to the event.

The barbeque was a huge success. The park was packed with men, women, and children, both Rochesterians and out-of-towners. The event was carefully organized, consisting of various food and product vendors, information tables for participating organizations, and game and exhibit areas.

Upon arrival, Kayla and Jasmine were hungry so Mrs. Simmons purchased everyone a barbeque dinner, complete with ribs, potato salad, baked beans, a couple slices of bread, and pop. Sitting at a green picnic table, they ate their food as they scoped out the scene and planned what they would do next. By the time everyone was full, Kayla and Jasmine had decided to go play Double Dutch, Mrs. Simmons was planning to go help set up the step show, and Ebony figured that she would go check out the informational tables and get some brochures on colleges and sororities.

Ebony began walking from table to table, perusing the literature available, taking pamphlets and freebies along the way. Although the Alphas and Deltas had impressive presentations and displays, the Zetas could not be outdone at their own event. They had sectioned off a large space of the park, having their tables form a huge Z. Blue and White balloons, streamers, tablecloths, pearls and other paraphernalia decorated the space. They were giving away free t-shirts, pencils, mugs, and baseball caps, drawing crowds of people to their tables hoping to get something free.

Ebony found herself engaged in an in-depth conversation about college with a Zeta sorority member who was attending the University of Rochester. The young woman loaded Ebony with brochures on the sorority, as well some of the free stuff everyone was dying to get. Ebony thanked the woman, promised to consider pledging Zeta in the future, and turned to walk away. As she turned, she crashed into someone who must have been standing directly behind her.

"Sorry!" she apologized quickly without looking up to see who she had just bumped into.

"Hey you!"

The voice sounded very familiar. Too familiar. She gazed upward, eyes bulging in disbelief. "Jaylen! What . . . What are you doing here?"

He smiled confidently. "I could say the same to you. But my cousin is a Zeta and she basically forced me to come, hoping maybe I would meet some of the Sigma brothers and let them talk me into going to college or something like that. I don't know. She is always trying to get me to go to college, but school ain't really for me."

She frowned briefly. "Why'd you say that? You could go to college. It's not a bad idea."

He turned away from the Zeta tables and began walking towards the picnic tables. She followed him, listening carefully to his reply. "I'm not like you, all smart and stuff. I mean, I thought about maybe going to trade school and getting my license to be a barber or fix cars, but I'm not sure if I really want to do that."

"Well, what do you want to do?" she asked, not taking her eyes away from him.

Nearing a green table, he sat down, his back against the table allowing him to observe the scenery. "I don't know. Still trying to figure that out. But I know I want to have my own business or something where I call the shots. I can't be working for nobody else. I don't do too well with people telling me what to do . . . So you never told me why you're here."

Ebony sat down next to him and scanned the park for her sister. "My sister's best friend's mother invited us. I really didn't want to come, but I had to be here with Kayla. Don't get me wrong. It's not that this isn't cool or that I'm not having a good time, but I'm just kind of tired from working and school and stuff like that. Been a long week.

"But I do like being around all these folks and seeing the sororities. I'm thinking about pledging one of them when I get to college. Not sure which one yet. Was looking at the AKA's at first, but now after meeting Jasmine's mom, Mrs. Simmons, I'm starting to like the Zetas. She is real cool and down to earth and all. And she is so smart. I think she got like two or three degrees! She always talking about what the Zetas are doing and the importance of getting a good education. She reminds me of my mom a little."

"Yeah, my cousin is always talking about the Zetas too! I'll have to introduce you to her. She's somewhere around here. So which one is your sister?"

She pointed in the direction of Kayla. "She's over there with those girls playing Double Dutch. She's the one with the yellow shirt and jean shorts."

Jaylen followed her hand and looked towards the games area. "I don't see . . . Oh, yeah, okay. I see her. She's a lot taller than I thought she'd be."

Ebony laughed. "She's twelve and a handful! But she's a good kid. She gets good grades in school and stays out of trouble for the most part."

Jaylen nodded his head. "So you spend a lot of time with her."

"Yeah, when I'm not working or at school. I have to. I'm all she got. I gotta make sure she doesn't do anything stupid to mess up her life."

Jaylen raised his eyebrows. "But you're only sixteen. That sounds like a huge responsibility for someone your age."

She shrugged. "It is, but hey, that's life . . . well at least what I've learned about it so far. It doesn't make sense and it ain't always fair. You just got to deal with it and make the best out of your situation."

"True, true. You're so serious, but I know it's cuz you got a lot that you been through. But you're strong, too. I like that."

Ebony didn't respond, but continued to look out into the crowd at all the families seemingly enjoying the barbeque. He thought she was strong while she thought she didn't want to be strong anymore. As she watched mothers and father embrace, laugh, and play with their children, sadness crept into her spirit. If only her mother could be there with her and Kayla then she wouldn't have to do so much. She could just be a kid; go to school, hang out, stuff that normal teens do. Instead she was stuck halfway between childhood and adulthood and the only thing that seemed to bring a smile to her face was the one thing she knew would only bring her more trouble: Jaylen.

September 10th

WHEN JAYLEN PULLED UP TO Edison Tech High school on Monday morning with Ebony in the car, Fawn almost flipped out. Fawn was leaning against the wall outside, talking to Ledell about why he didn't call her back last night when she spotted Ebony getting out of Jaylen's car.

"Oh, heck no!" Fawn yelled, making Ledell even more nervous.

"Dag, I didn't think a phone call was that serious!" Ledell said defensively.

"Forget the phone call, Dell! Look at that idiot over there getting out of old dude's car!" Fawn exclaimed while crossing her arms and directing her attention to the drop-off loop.

"Who?" Ledell said confused about Fawn's change in topic.

"Ebony! She over there getting out of that drug dealer Jaylen's car."

Ledell, finally noticing Ebony walking away from an unfamiliar vehicle, caught on to what Fawn was ranting about. "She's messing with him?"

"She better not be. Hold up." Fawn walked a few steps closer to the parking lot and waved her arms, signaling for Ebony to join her and Ledell. "Ebony! Ebony! Come here!"

Here we go, Ebony thought as she made her way towards her best friend. "Hey y'all. It's kind of chilly out here today, ain't it?" Ebony said trying to act normal.

"I bet it is chilly after you just got out of Jaylen's warm car," Fawn snapped.

Ebony sucked her teeth. "What? Girl, you trippin."

Fawn put her hands on her hips. "No 'E,' you're the one trippin'. I thought we already discussed this! Why you hanging with that rock slinger?"

"You don't even know him. And last time I checked, my momma's name was not Fawn." Ebony tried to keep herself calm. She thought she was prepared to hear Fawn's trash talking, but suddenly, she found herself extremely irritated.

"I ain't tryin' to be ya momma, I'm trying to be your friend," Fawn pleaded.

Ebony watched Jaylen's car move further and further away from the school. When she could no long see the car in the distance, she hesitantly turned her attention to her best friend. "Fawn, you know you my girl, but my relationship with Jaylen really isn't any of your business. Do I tell you what to do about Ledell?"

"Ledell don't sell drugs, and if he did then I would expect you to tell me to let him go." Fawn replied coldly, unwilling to understand Ebony's perspective.

"Why I got to be selling drugs?" Ledell interrupted.

Fawn playfully pushed Ledell then redirected her attention to the matter at hand. "Ebony, this dude is not what you think. You deserve better. Plus I don't want you getting caught up in his mess."

Ebony was offended. "You think I'm stupid or something? What? You think I'm gonna start using drugs now? Or better yet, you think I'm going start selling for him?"

"I'm not saying that, I'm saying–," Fawn started, but was cut off by Ebony.

"Fawn, you've already said enough. Now let me make something clear. Jaylen is my man and we are going to be together whether or not you like it. So deal with it. I'm out; I got to get to class." Ebony rolled her eyes and walked into the building leaving Fawn and Ledell behind.

She hated that her friend and her were arguing, but Fawn had no right to try to regulate her relationship like that. Fawn didn't know anything about Jaylen. Yeah, he wasn't perfect, but he was a sweetheart and treated her with respect. Bump what anyone thought; it was her life and she was going to live it her way.

Ebony was happy to see Jaylen's car waiting for her when the final bell rang. The day had seemed longer than usual since she was unable to chill with Fawn during lunch or in the halls. She was already regretting her fight with her best friend, but at the same time she felt that Fawn had overstepped her boundary. When she got in the car, she immediately told Jaylen about her day and her argument with Fawn.

"I'm sorry to hear that, but you can't let your friends run your life," Jaylen said once she finished giving him the details about their disagreement.

Ebony sat back in the seat. "I know; it's just that she is my best friend and I hate that fact that we're fighting."

"Well, don't even worry about that. You are with me now and I'm gonna make you feel better."

She smiled and said, "Oh really?"

With confidence he answered, "Fo' sho! I need to run over to my man's house real quick and pick up something and then maybe we can chill. You smoke?"

"Smoke what?" she asked, but she already knew the answer.

"Trees," he replied with no hesitation.

"Nah, do you?" She knew the answer to this question too.

"Of course. It's what keeps me sane."

She turned her body towards him and asked, "What you mean by that?"

He turned down the music and looked at her seriously. "Check it! I got a hard life to live. My dad's a crack head, my mom works three jobs just to take care of my four sisters and brothers, a few of my boys have been killed and the ones who are still alive are all locked up. I'm out here trying to hustle to take care of myself and throw mom dukes a couple dollars. Then I got people like your friend Fawn always judging me when they ain't walked a day in my shoes. Her parents living like the Jeffersons! I'm just trying to survive. I don't smoke every day, but sometimes, I just need something to take the edge off, you know?"

She felt bad for him. She had no clue he was going through so much. "I can relate. I work at Burger World 'cause my grandmother can't afford to take care of me and my sister."

"See, that's why I like you. You understand me. You're not like the rest of these people out here trying to down a brotha . . . I want to take you somewhere."

"Where?" Ebony asked curiously.

"You'll see."

Ebony thought for a second about her plans for the day. "But I am supposed to be at the football game tonight to pass out flyers and sell tickets for ABLE's AIDS benefit."

He rubbed her knee and said, "I'll get you to your game on time, don't worry."

They drove around town for an hour, making stops here and there to take care of Jaylen's "business." Finally, Jaylen took Ebony to Irondequoit Bay, a beach on Lake Ontario. Jaylen sat behind Ebony on a giant rock, wrapping his arms and legs around hers. The view was beautiful: soft waves rolling onto the shore, a clear blue sky that seemed to extend forever beyond the water, seagulls flying overhead making their presence known through their call. For the first time in a long time

Ebony felt at peace. Here there weren't money issues, no school or work responsibilities, no thoughts about the safety of her sister. Here it was just Jaylen, her, and the enormous lake.

Jaylen pulled out a pre-rolled blunt and lit it up. "You don't mind, do you?" he asked.

"No, you cool," Ebony responded.

"Man, I love coming out here. When things get crazy, I just come here, smoke some trees, and let it all go."

"Yeah it is relaxing." Ebony looked curiously at Jaylen as he puffed on the blunt and appeared to become mellower. "Does weed really make you feel calmer?"

Jaylen chuckled. "Does it! Baby, if it wasn't for marijuana, I would have killed someone or myself by now. For real!" He looked at her carefully, noticing the interest in her eyes. "What? You wanna hit this? Jaylen said extending the blunt to Ebony.

She was curious. Although she knew it was the wrong thing to do, a part of her wanted to experience the peace and tranquility that Jaylen spoke about.

"I shouldn't . . ."

"You sure? It'll make you feel better."

"Umm . . . nah, I'm cool." she said with uncertainty.

"Okay, it's your choice." Jaylen stood up and walked down the beach as he continued smoking. Ebony stared out into the lake's bluish-brown water, allowing her thoughts to run endlessly through her mind. She thought about her mom and how much she missed her. She thought about ABLE and their upcoming event. She thought about her fight with Fawn and how bossy Fawn could be. She thought about her sister and what she needed to do to protect her. And she thought about Jaylen, about how good it felt to have someone special in her life.   Unintentionally,   she glanced over at him and instantly became aware of him gazing at her. She smiled and looked away, embarrassed by his attentiveness. He took one last drag from the blunt and tossed the remaining paper into the lake. After watching the brown paper hit the water and begin to float atop of it, he began walking back over towards Ebony. Reclaiming his seat on the boulder behind her, he enclosed her in his arms, pulling her close to him as if his life depended on it. Ebony allowed herself to be enveloped in the tranquil aromatic mixture of marijuana and Men's Guess cologne. His arms felt secure and safe and for the first time in a really long time she let down her guard.

They talked and they talked and although she knew she had somewhere to be, she refused to let the moment end. At that moment, she didn't care about ABLE, Fawn, or anything else. All that mattered was Jaylen's touch and his comforting words. He listened when she spoke and his response was always positive and encouraging. He didn't treat her like she was naïve or young; he treated her like she was the most delicate and fascinating woman in the world. It was the most romantic evening of her life, but like all good things, it came to an end.

At 9 o'clock, he dropped her off at home. She ran to her room, not wanting to deal with her grandmother or Kayla. After taking a shower, she listened to the few messages she had on her voicemail.

Message one: Hey girl, it's Alisa. I'm down here at the football game with the crew. We are waiting on you to help us with the flyers and tickets. I hope you haven't forgotten. Call me or come on down.

Message two: It's Fawn. So I guess you are so mad at me that you have just walked away from your responsibilities at ABLE. You're supposed to be here at the game and I bet you are out with that fool somewhere. Call me back.

Message three: It's Fawn again. Look, I am really sorry if I offended you earlier, but I am really starting to get worried about you. This is not like you at all. Please call me back.

End of voicemail.

"Dag!" Ebony said aloud to herself. She had gotten so wrapped up with Jaylen that she'd forgotten about the game. "Oh, well. Nothing I can do about it now.

They'll be alright," Ebony tried to convince herself. She would wait until tomorrow to talk to Fawn. She had a perfect evening with Jaylen and didn't want to spoil it by fussing with her. She fell asleep thinking about her wonderful time at the beach.

September 11th

EBONY HAD BEEN AVOIDING Fawn all day and had managed to make it to lunch without running into her. She really did not want to hear Fawn's nagging. As much as she loved Fawn and valued her friendship, she hated that Fawn was a straight control freak. Fawn always acted like she was Ebony's mother, always telling her what to do and what not to do. If they were going to stay friends, Fawn would have to chill out. Not only that, but Fawn was going to have to accept Jaylen. She was really starting to fall for him and wasn't willing to give him up because of Fawn's disapproval.

Ebony was sitting in the lunchroom watching Petey and Rome, two Edison Tech seniors, hustle some freshmen out of their money during a spades game when Fawn finally caught up with her.

"There you are! I've been looking for you all day! What happened to you last night?" Fawn said loudly as she walked up to her in the school's cafeteria.

Ebony laughed as Rome slammed a card down on the table and scraped up another book the team had won. "Girl, I was just tired and decided to stay in, you know?"

Fawn stood above her and glared down at her, irritated by her nonchalance. "No I don't know. Why don't you explain it to me?"

"Explain what Fawn?" Ebony said calmly, still not looking up from the table.

"Why you're acting all funny," Fawn huffed.

Ebony glanced over her shoulder, back at Fawn. "I said I was tired."

Fawn crossed her arms, unsure of how to deal with her defiant friend. This was so unlike the Ebony she knew. That was the problem. She didn't know the girl sitting in front of her. "What's up with you? You never cancel on us without at least calling. You didn't answer your phone and you didn't even call me back."

Annoyed, Ebony turned around all the way in her seat to face Fawn. "Fawn, what is this? An FBI investigation? Why are you in interrogating me? Dag, I said I was tired, end of story! Let it go."

Fawn stared hard and her, mystified by her behavior. "Ebony I don't know who you are anymore. This is not the Ebony that has been my best friend for the past two years."

Ebony was tired of talking and through with explaining herself to Fawn. She stood up, bringing her face inches away from Fawn's. She was so close to Fawn that she could smell the Johnson Baby Powder that Fawn faithfully poured down her shirt every morning to keep her from smelling sweaty. "Well, maybe you just didn't know me as well as you thought you did."

"Maybe you're right," Fawn responded hopelessly.

Ebony smirked at Fawn's desperation to control her then turned her back to Fawn and walked away, leaving Fawn standing in the center of the cafeteria, dumbfounded.

WEDNESDAY'S ABLE MEETING WAS certainly awkward, but looking at Ebony, one would have never guessed it. She sat (apart from Fawn) in the front of the room, her eyes fully focused on the podium, appearing to be completely interested in the meeting's happenings. Although everyone was aware that Ebony had been a no-show to the football game where she was expected to pass out tickets, Ebony participated in the group conversation, offering her ideas freely as if she was one-hundred percent committed to the event. Meanwhile, Fawn sat further back in the room in their usual spot next to Desiree and Latoya, glaring at the back of Ebony's head, rolling her eyes every time she spoke. This behavior went unnoticed to most of the

ABLE members; however, with Alisa's being at the front podium during most of the meeting, her view of the room was unique and therefore she was able to witness the odd behavior of the two ex-best friends.

When the meeting adjourned, Alisa took it upon herself to get to the bottom of the strange behavior, starting first with Ebony.

As Ebony stuffed her notes into her book bag, Alisa hurriedly made her way to the empty seat next to her. Ebony felt Alisa's approach, smelled the scent of her designer fragrance, but pretended she wasn't there. Ebony knew that Alisa could be a bit nosy so she figured she probably wanted to find out why Ebony and Fawn weren't sitting together. If Alisa wanted to talk, Alisa would have to make the first move. As far as Ebony was concerned, Alisa needed to say something quickly because Ebony was headed out of the door.

It wasn't until Ebony zipped up her bag that Alisa finally found the gumption to speak. "Hey E. What's going on?"

"Alisa. Nothing much." Ebony's tone was flat and unemotional.

Feeling a bit anxious, Alisa shifted in the chair. "I called you the other night, the night of the game. Did you get my message?"

"Ummm. Yeah. I believe so," Ebony responded.

"Well, it was strange that you didn't make it to the game and we didn't hear from you. Is everything okay?"

Alisa made eye contact with Ebony, searching for a hint or glimmer of emotion. Ebony continued to offer none.

"I'm fine. Just got caught up with something else that I needed to handle, that's all."

Alisa forced a smile. "I understand. We all have a life, right?"

"Right."

Alisa was getting nowhere fast. If she wanted answers, she would need to be direct and blunt. And that's exactly what she did next. "I don't mean to be all up in your business, but is everything okay between you and Fawn. You two are usually like Siamese twins, completely inseparable. But tonight it seems as if there is some tension . . . between you two. For real, what's up?"

Ebony smirked at Alisa's desperate attempts to play peacemaker, but she still wasn't willing to let Alisa in. "People go through stuff, Alisa, even friends. It's nothing Fawn and I can't figure out on our own."

Alisa gave up. Ebony was hard as a rock. It was best to just to leave her alone. "Point taken. Well, I hope you figure it out soon. Good friends are few and far in between. Have a good night," Alisa replied as she stood up and began to walk away.

"You too," Ebony said quickly then darted towards the door.

Alisa watched Ebony make her speedy getaway, wondering what Ebony was hiding. Although she pretended to let it go, secretly she planned to find out what was really going on. Something didn't feel right about Ebony's behavior. Alisa's intuition tugged at her: Ebony was in trouble. Fawn was preoccupied, talking to

Ledell and Ms. Washington, but Alisa made herself a mental note to talk to her as soon as possible. As soon as possible turned out to be the very next day.

September 13th

EBONY CRINGED AS SHE FLIPPED over the graded math test. D+. The evil letter mocked her. Ebony was an A/B student and although math was somewhat challenging for her, she could always manage to obtain a good grade on every assignment and every test. Yes, she had studied a little less for this test, but a D? *Seriously?* she thought. She flipped the paper back over to prevent herself from crying. *What else could go wrong? Life is so unfair.*

The phone rang twice before Alisa heard Fawn's voice.

"Fawn? Hey, what's up? This is Alisa . . . No, I'm cool and everything is good with ABLE. I just want to talk to you. I noticed that you and Ebony weren't sitting together at the meeting yesterday and when I went to talk to her she seemed a little distant. Is everything ok? . . . Oh for real? . . . Wow, that's crazy! . . . Well, I am so sorry to hear that, but we cannot let her lose herself in this guy. Girls do that all the time and end up in some bad situations. . . Just leave her alone for now until we can figure out a way to deal with this appropriately. If you keep talking to her, it's just going to make things worse. . . We should talk to Ms. Washington about this and maybe she can help us come up with a plan. . . I'm supposed to meet with her at the Eastman Theater on Monday to go over the details with their management about the talent show. Can you meet us up there around 4:30? . . . Okay, great! See you on Monday." Alisa hung up her end of the phone and sighed. "Drama."

September 14th

ON FRIDAY, FAWN AND LEDELL ALMOST walked past Ebony in the hallway at school as if they didn't know her. Almost. At the last moment, Ledell looked back, giving her a look that said, "I'm sorry. We're still cool, but Fawn won't let me speak to you."

Fawn's eyes never turned in Ebony's direction. For the first time since she'd moved to Rochester, Ebony knew what it felt like to be an outsider. Ebony made a mental note: Find new friends.

September 15th

ON SATURDAY, EBONY FOUND herself back at Irondequoit Beach, enjoying the sounds of the tiny, crashing waves and the closeness of Jaylen's embrace. She needed someone to talk to about everything that was going on in her life, but with her and Fawn being on bad terms, the only person she felt comfortable with was Jaylen. In her mind, he was so nonjudgmental, so willing to just accept her, flaws and all. She didn't have to pretend she was perfect; she didn't have to have it all together.

As she sat on the huge boulder and rested the top of her head against his chest, she replayed the last few years of her life in her mind. Pictorial glimpses of both happy and sad moments flashed rapidly, causing her to do something that she hadn't planned on doing; she began to cry. She tried to take a few deep breaths to calm down and stop the tears, but it was pointless. They rebelliously continued to fall.

Noticing her distress, Jaylen pulled her closer. "Baby, what's wrong?" he asked sympathetically.

She couldn't respond for fear that the pain would increase. Somehow, he understood her silence and didn't probe her with any more questions. They sat quietly, listening to the sounds of the lake and nature which surrounded them.

Eventually Ebony was able to control her breathing and her tears. When she finally found the words, she turned to Jalyen and said, "Sorry for being so emotional, I just–."
He interrupted her. "You don't have to apologize. We all got to let off some steam sometimes."

She sighed in relief. "Thanks for being cool about it. Sometimes it just feels like the whole world is just caving in on me, like I can't handle it all."

"I feel you."

She exhaled. "I know you do. . . I miss my best friend, but I am so tired of trying to please everybody, fit into everyone's expectation of me. I feel like I just can't be myself because I have to be my sister's mother, a good student, a dependable employee, a perfect friend, and the list goes on. I just want to be sixteen!" Ebony exclaimed.

He looked at her sternly and said, "Then just be sixteen. You only have to be what you want to be. Nobody is stopping you, but you."

Jaylen's words sound so simple to Ebony. *Just be sixteen*. She repeated to words in her thoughts, each time the phrase having more power.

Jaylen sighed, reached into his denim pocket, and pulled out a pre-made blunt. He lit the cigar with a transparent blue lighter and began to smoke as Ebony watched him curiously. She knew it was wrong, but Jaylen seemed so peaceful, so confident, so clear-minded, and she could not help but long to feel that way too.

"Can I?" she asked, almost surprised at the words coming out of her mouth.

"This?" he asked as he extended the drug towards her. "You sure?" he hesitated, astonished by the request.

She looked at him then at the rolled brown paper he was holding and said, "Yeah."

He shrugged his shoulders and passed the blunt to her. Ebony smiled faintly then attempted to imitate his smoking style. The first puff she was able to intake with ease, but by the second, she inhaled too much and began to cough as the smoke filled and irritated her lungs. "Slow down, Shorty!" Jaylen said as he laughed at her amateurish ways.

She giggled and tried again, watching him as he nodded in approval. Once she had gotten the hang of it, she passed the blunt back to Jaylen, allowing him to share the experience with her.

They sat on the rock and smoked and talked for hours. He was right, she was calm and at peace. Her cell phone went off a few times, but she ignored it, not wanting to be distracted from the serene feeling she was experiencing. *So this is what life is supposed to feel like*, she thought, pulling him closer. At that moment she decided that she wanted every day to feel like that day, peaceful and free . . . even if it meant taking on a new hobby: smoking marijuana.

September 16th

DESPITE KAYLA'S CONSTANT NAGGING, on Sunday, Ebony refused to get out of bed and do . . . anything. They were supposed to go to church, wash and re-braid Kayla's hair, and catch a matinee movie, but none of it happened. After Kayla stormed in and out of Ebony's room for the 100th time, Ebony got up, locked her door, and turned her cellular phone's ringer off. When Kayla approached Ebony's room for the 101st time, she was greeted by a locked door. Kayla, being determined, commenced to knocking hard, non-stop. Ebony, being the older and smarter sibling, shoved a pair of earphones in her ears, turned her MP3 player up as loud as it would go, and returned peacefully back to sleep.

"What is going on up here?" Mamma Dee demanded when the knocking became annoying.

"Ebony locked her door and won't get up! We were supposed to go to church and the movies today! And my hair is a mess! I can't go to school like this tomorrow! She won't get up! Make her get up!"

Momma Dee sighed and turned towards the closed, oak, wooden door. "Ebony, Ebony," she called out into the door.

There was no response.

"See grandma!" Kayla cried.

"Listen, Kayla. Yo' sister is just tired. She got a lot goin' on. You let her rest."

"But what about my hair?" Kayla whined.

"I'll call Pam across the street and have her do yo' hair. It ain't the end of the world Kayla."

Kayla poked out her bottom lip and stormed towards her bedroom. Momma Dee sighed again, unsure of what to think about Ebony's abnormal behavior. But Ebony was just a child and Momma Dee understood that some things were just a part of growing up. She prayed that this was just one of those things.

September 17th

WHEN FAWN WALKED INTO the Eastman
Theater on Monday, Alisa and Ms. Washington were
wrapping up their meeting with the theater's assistant
manager. Alisa was leaning over a large table reviewing
a map of the facility as Ms. Washington stood directly
in front of the assistant manager, engaged in
conversation. Upon hearing Fawn's entrance, Alisa
looked up and gestured to Fawn, letting her know that
they would be done soon. Fawn nodded to let Alisa
know she understood her gesture then took a seat in the
vestibule on a medium-sized, formal, Victorian-style
sofa.

As Fawn waited, she allowed her mind to drift off
to thoughts about her friendship with Ebony. They had

become friends when they were in elementary school and Ebony's mom used to bring her up to Rochester during the summers to visit her grandmother. Although they lived in different states, the girls remained close friends and communicated often, initially through phone calls and letters, then later through email and text messaging. When Ebony's mother died and Kayla and Ebony relocated to Rochester permanently, Fawn and Ebony were reunited as best friends. Since Fawn was a year older than Ebony, she always assumed more of an older sister role in their relationship. Until recently, Ebony never complained about Fawn's meddling behaviors. It was understood that if one of them were making a bad decision the other would be honest and confront her, pulling no punches. But now that Ebony was with Jaylen, she no longer seemed to want Fawn to "keep it real" with her.

Fawn shook her head as she thought about how stupidly Ebony was behaving. She would have never suspected Ebony of all people to get caught up in a guy and start acting funny. There were girls who became real "remedial" when it came to boys, but Fawn would have never thought that Ebony would be one of those girls, until now.

Ten minutes later, Alisa and Ms. Washington approached the sofa where Fawn was patiently waiting. Alisa sat down next to Fawn, being sure to smooth out her green and brown plaid skirt as she did so. *So Alisa!* Ms. Washington also took a seat, easing slowly onto the gray wingback chair that faced the Victorian sofa.

"Hi Fawn," Ms. Washington greeted her as she sat back and crossed her legs.

Fawn smiled and eyed the 30-something year old woman's sharp, black and white pinstriped, business suit. "Hello, Ms. Washington. You look nice today."

"Well thank you!" Ms. Washington replied while looking down at her clothes. "So what's going on ladies? You all wanted to talk to me about something?"

Fawn looked at Alisa who then decided to start the conversation. "Yeah, we got a little situation. It seems as if Ebony has been acting a little strangely lately and we are concerned that she might be getting involved with the wrong type of people."

Ms. Washington glanced at Fawn who nodded her head in agreement. "Okay. So tell me more."

Fawn slid towards the edge of the sofa so that she could get closer to Ms. Washington. "Well, about two weeks ago I found out she was associating with this guy named Jaylen who is known for being a drug dealer. When I questioned her about him, she got an attitude with me. I noticed she was acting weirdly, but Ebony has been through a lot so I thought it was about her mom or something like that. But then one day she shows up to school in his car and says that they are a couple. She missed the football game where she was supposed to help us sell tickets for the talent show and she has basically written me off as a friend because I don't agree with her dating Jaylen.

"To make matters worse, her sister called me yesterday and said that she refused to get out of bed and hang out with her on Sunday. That is so unlike Ebony. No matter what, she always looks out for her sister. I am really afraid that this guy has gotten all in her head and who knows what he has her doing? She might even be using drugs!"

Alisa shook her head in disbelief. "No, no way. Do you really think she would let it go that far?"

Fawn shrugged her shoulders. "I don't know what to think because I don't know this Ebony! It's like she's a completely different person! She talks to me like I'm nothing. I'm her best friend!"

"Ladies, don't assume the worst. Let us try to be positive about this. It's natural for young women to get a little confused when they first start dating. And with everything that Ebony has been through, I am sure she is still dealing with a lot of pain."

Filled with emotion, Fawn stood up and said, "So what do we do? Just let her throw her life away?

"No, I am not recommending that, but you need to understand that we can't force her to do anything she doesn't want to do. If she likes this guy and decides she wants to be with him, we cannot stop her. Have you ever heard of the expression, 'You catch more flies with honey'?"

Alisa's eyebrows narrowed. "No, that's a new one. What does it mean?"

"It means that you are more likely to get someone's attention through being kind and gentle with them than being impatient and cold. I will talk with her at Wednesday's meeting, but in the meantime I need you two to be supportive of her," Ms. Washington replied.

Fawn fell back onto the sofa in frustration, apparently unhappy with Ms. Washington's advice. Alisa attempted to console her by rubbing her right arm softly.

Ms. Washington frowned and said, "I know it's not easy to watch your friend head down the wrong road, but she is growing into a woman and she has to learn how to make wise choices. Unfortunately, sometimes we have to mess up a few times before we get it right."

"I know, Ms. Washington. I just hate that there's nothing I can do," Fawn whimpered.

"But you are doing something. You are helping your friend by seeking help and supporting her by loving her despite your personal feelings about her behavior," Ms. Washington responded.

Alisa continued to rub Fawn's arm and said, "Ms. Washington is right. Being a good friend means sticking by the people we love even when we don't like their choices."

Fawn looked back and forth from Alisa's face to Ms. Washington's face, both of them waiting for her to give in. "Okay, okay. I will try to be more supportive. I really hope this works because if it doesn't, I might have to put Ebony in a headlock!"

Alisa and Ms. Washington laughed at Fawn's idle threat, but she didn't even crack a smile. As far as Fawn was concerned, she was willing to do whatever it took to keep Ebony safe.

September 18ᵗʰ

TUESDAY AFTER SCHOOL, Ebony hung out with Jaylen again. Instead of going to their spot at the beach, he flaunted his new girl in front of a few of his friends at an eastside barbershop named "Blades and Fades." Located on Thurston Road near Chili Avenue, "Blades and Fades" was owned by a tall, dark-skinned man known as "Loco" who also happened to be Jaylen's cousin.

Ebony sat on one of the empty barber chairs and listened enthusiastically as the males in the shop laughed and joked about everything from politics to prices. Periodically, one of Jaylen's "boys" or "customers" would walk into the shop; have a private conversation with Jaylen, and then exit the building, but not before publicly complimenting Jaylen on his "cute" girlfriend.

At one point in the evening, Jaylen turned to Ebony and said, "We about to go out back and fire one up. You down?"

Ebony, completely engrossed in the whole barbershop experience, quickly agreed and followed him out the back door which led to a small, dimly lit alley. Although she was still slightly uncomfortable with smoking, she watched carefully as the freshly rolled blunt was passed between Jaylen and two of the barbershop's employees. When the "herb" was finally passed in her direction, Ebony offered a pseudo confident smile, reached out her hand, and hoped she wouldn't end up looking like a rookie.

September 19th

AFTER WEDNESDAY'S ABLE MEETING, Ms. Washington had every intention on remaining true to her promise to Fawn and having some "girl talk" with Ebony. But there was only one problem: Ebony was a no show.

September 20th

ON THURSDAY, EBONY DID SOMETHING that she never did before: she skipped school.

She never meant to skip, it just sort of happened. She had missed Wednesday's ABLE meeting because she was hanging out again at the barbershop with Jaylen and lost track of time. By the time she looked at the clock on her cell phone, the meeting was half over. She could only imagine the thoughts Fawn was thinking about her, but it really didn't matter. Jaylen was quickly becoming her new best friend and Fawn's friendship was unavoidably becoming obsolete.

After Jaylen dropped her off at home (around 9 p.m.), he called her and they stayed on the phone until three in the morning, when her cell phone battery could take no more. Of course, on Thursday, she overslept. Momma Dee had a doctor's appointment and wasn't there to wake her up or make sure she had left for school on time. Kayla was still upset with her for flaking on Sunday and refused to talk to her much less wake her up for school.

So when Ebony cracked open her eyes and realized that she'd forgotten to set her alarm clock and now was thirty minutes late for school, she quickly dialed Jaylen's number and asked him for a ride. He told her that he would be there in thirty minutes.

He got there an hour later.

Now an hour and a half late, Ebony was stressed. She ran and jumped into his car as if she was fleeing the scene after robbing a bank. "I can't believe I overslept!" Ebony shrieked.

"Calm down babe," Jaylen insisted. "What's done is done. You cannot do anything about it now."

Ebony looked over at Jaylen who for some crazy reason always seemed to be so calm and collected. *It must be so nice not to have a care in the world*, she thought. She took a deep breath and looked out the window, not wanting to overwhelm him with her anxiety.

He glanced over at her as he pulled away from the curb and began in route towards Edison Tech High. "Whatcha thinking?" he asked as he made left at the first intersection.

She gazed at his cool demeanor and sighed. "I just wish I could be more like you, so worry-free."

He laughed. "Are you stressed out, love?"

She smiled and nodded, feeling vulnerable and foolish.

"Well, if you want, we can go roll one before you go to school. That's what I do when I'm stressed. But then again, it would make you even later for school," he replied then looked at her to see her reaction.

Ebony paused and thought about her options. *I'm already late for school and I'm a nervous wreck. I have another math exam today and I'm in no mood to take it. If I go straight to school now, I know I will fail. I'm too tense! But if I go smoke with Jaylen, it will give me time to chill out a little and maybe I can do better on the test*, she rationalized. After talking to herself for a minute or two she finally turned to Jaylen and said, "Can we go to the beach?"

Somehow, she never did get to school or take the math test.

September 21st

EBONY WAS PUTTING HER science book in her locker when Fawn approached her the next day. Fawn was livid that Ebony had missed Wednesday's ABLE meeting and even angrier that she hadn't seen Ebony in school on Thursday; however, she decided to take the advice of Ms. Washington and try to be supportive.

"Ebony?" Fawn said nervously as she walked closer to the gray, open locker door.

Ebony turned her head slightly to acknowledge that she heard Fawn, but didn't reply back.

Be supportive, Fawn reminded herself. "How have you been?" Fawn asked attempting to sound as pleasant as possible.

Ebony grabbed the navy blue English book from the top shelf of her locker and slammed the locker door shut. "I'm fine."

Fawn forced herself to smile. "Good. I'm glad to hear that. . . Uh, we missed you at the ABLE meeting."

"Yeah, I was busy," Ebony said dryly.

Supportive, Fawn repeated to herself once more. "Well, uh, we were just finalizing everything for the talent show. You know it's next Saturday, right?"

"I remember."

"Are you *still* going to participate?"

"Why wouldn't I?"

Fawn bit her lip, unsure of how to keep up the charade. "Oh, okay, well you've just been a little M.I.A. lately." She sighed and continued, "Look Ebony, we've been friends almost our whole lives. I hate not talking to you, it's just . . ."

Ebony rolled her eyes. "It's just you don't like my boyfriend and want me to leave him alone. It's just you don't think I'm smart enough to make my own decisions."

"No, girl it's not like that. I mean, yes, I don't care for Jaylen, but I do care about you and I do think you're smart. You are just not being smart right now with this situation," Fawn pleaded.

Ebony laughed, but more out of disbelief than humor. "I'm not being smart because I won't do what you want me to do. Is that what it is?"

Fawn couldn't take her attitude anymore. *Bump supportive!* she thought to herself. "No, you're not being smart because you can't see that this guy is all up in your head, got your nose wide open! You are not even yourself anymore."

Ebony's eyebrows raised in curiosity. "What do you know about me doing me?"

Fawn put her hands on her hips and replied, "I know that Ebony, the real Ebony, wouldn't abandon her little sister over a dude."

"Whatever!" Ebony pointed in Fawn's face. "You need to get a life and stay out of mine." She rolled her eyes again, turned, and walked away in the opposite direction.

Fawn stood there frozen and frustrated, watching her ex-best friend grow smaller and smaller as she faded out into the distance.

September 22nd

ON SATURDAY, ABLE HELD auditions for the talent show in the auditorium at the School of the Arts. Over fifty acts showed up in hopes of landing one of the fifteen performance slots included in the show. The performances included individual and group musical numbers, drama, dance, poetry, stepping, comedy routines, magic routines, and a bunch of other weird and creative acts that kids had learned to do.

The panel of judges included Alisa, Fawn, Desiree, Ledell, Omar, and Trenton. Ms. Washington and Mr. Armstrong were also in attendance to help keep the auditions organized and running smoothly.

Halfway through the auditions, the judges were permitted to take a fifteen minute break to stretch and use the bathroom. In the ladies room, Fawn, Alisa, and Desiree gathered to get an update on the whole Ebony drama.

"Have you seen Ebony lately?" Alisa asked while squeezing the soap dispenser and lathering her hands with the pearl colored soap.

Fawn fixed her hair in the mirror, not that anything was really wrong with it to start. "Not really. I didn't see her on Thursday, but I did run into her in front of the lockers on Friday."

Alisa turned on the faucet and began to rinse off her soapy hands. "So how did that go?"

Fawn stopped playing with her hair and turned towards Alisa who was still washing her hands. "Horrible. I tried the whole supportive thing, but she was just being difficult. I was so ready to slap some sense into her, I swear."

Desiree emerged from the far left stall and approached the sinks to wash her hands. "Who are y'all talking about? Ebony? What's going on with her? I haven't seen her in a while."

Fawn leaned against the sink. "Ebony is straight trippin'. She's been dating this dude and he got her looking like a fool."

Desiree shook her wet hands. "Not Ebony! For real?"

"Yes, my girl! I am so hot about it!" Fawn exclaimed.

"I bet you are. So, who is this guy? Do I know him? Someone in ABLE?" Desiree asked as she dried her hands with a paper towel.

Fawn stood up straight and shook her head. "No, no. It's this dude named Jaylen. He's not in high school anymore."

Desiree looked at her in shock. "You mean Jaylen Tisdale? The . . . you know?"

"Yes! That's the one. The street pharmacist," Alisa interjected.

Desiree was stunned. "Oh wow! How did she get mixed up with him?"

"I really don't know, but she is in real deep. She won't listen to anything I say," Fawn responded, obviously irritated.

Alisa walked towards the bathroom door then paused before she opened it. "I know you're upset about this whole thing Fawn, but Ms. Washington was right the other day. We can't control her. She is going to have to be a big girl and figure this thing out on her own. We just have to hope that she is as smart as we thought she was and be here when it all falls apart."

Fawn exhaled in defeat. "Yeah. Let's just pray that when it does, she doesn't get pulled down with it."

September 23rd

AFTER THE PREVIOUS SUNDAY'S disappointment, Kayla didn't even attempt to wake Ebony the following Sunday. Ebony rolled out of bed and almost freaked out when the digital numbers informed her that it was already 1 o'clock in the afternoon. The truth is that although sleeping in last Sunday had been a nice change, she missed hanging out with her little sister and felt guilty about dissing her.

Ebony pushed the lilac comforter off of her body and swung her legs over the side of the bed, forcing herself to get up. She slid her feet into a pair of comfy, red slippers and pulled her body into a standing position. She could hear the sounds of Momma Dee downstairs in the kitchen cooking Sunday dinner which was always slammin'. Just the thought of greens, black eyed peas, fried chicken, cornbread, and peach cobbler made Ebony's mouth water.

Ebony shook the thoughts of dinner out of her mind and refocused back on the task of reuniting with her sister. She opened her bedroom door and yelled down the hallway, hoping to get Kayla to come to her. "Kayla! Kayla!" There was no response. Lazily, she dragged her body down to Kayla's room and peered inside. Kayla wasn't there. *Maybe she's downstairs with Momma Dee*, she thought.

Ebony returned to her room, wrapped her black, terry cloth robe around her and proceeded downstairs to the kitchen. The closer she got to the kitchen, the more intense the smells of hot grease, steaming vegetables, and baking bread became. By the time she reached the kitchen she knew she would need a snack to hold her over until dinnertime. The enticing aromas reminded her that she hadn't eaten since Saturday afternoon.

She entered the kitchen, kissed Momma Dee on her cheek and instantly headed for the refrigerator.

"Where's Kayla?" she asked while opening its door and searching its contents for something she could munch on.

"She's with Jasmine and her mother," Momma Dee responded while stirring the greens she was cooking in a big, black pot.

"Oh." Ebony was disappointed, but managed to say, "That's cool." She pulled a giant pickle out of a humongous jar and wrapped it in a paper towel before biting down on it.

Momma Dee put the lid back on the pot and allowed the food to simmer again. Turning towards Ebony and her giant pickle, she felt it was a good time to talk to Ebony. She had noticed that lately Ebony had been acting strangely—coming home later than normal, always being tired and hungry, more irritable and less social, being unconcerned with her sister's needs—and she knew that it was time to put Ebony in check. Although Ebony was developing into a little lady, she still was just a child and needed guidance and direction. Momma Dee didn't scold the girls often, but her parental instincts told her that this was one of those occasions when Ebony needed to experience some "tough love."

"Ebony," Momma Dee said to get her attention.

"Yes ma'am," Ebony replied before taking another bite of the sweet yet salty pickle.

"I know you're getting older and going through a lot of changes, but I still 'spect for you to do what's right and 'member what's important."

Ebony backed up to the counter and leaned back against it, preparing herself for a lecture.

Momma Dee pointed at her with the large spoon she had been using to stir the greens. "Now, you've been acting unlike yo'self the last few weeks. You ain't been nice to yo' sister, coming in the house not speakin' to anyone, always wanna sleep, that's not like you. Now what I suspect is that you must got yo'self a little boyfriend. That's the only thing that make a smart, young girl act silly."

Ebony remained silent. She shifted her body against the counter and lowered her eyes to the ground.

"You don't have to tell me what's goin' on or if you got yo'self a friend, but let me give you some advice. A lot of these young men out here are selfish, they all about themselves. If a guy really cares about you, he will make sure that what you value and what's important to you will be a priority. You shouldn't have to give up what is good about you just to be with him. Now that's all I'ma say 'bout it. You just make sure that you don't let no one stop you from making something positive out of yo' life. You hear me?"

"Yes ma'am," Ebony said, still looking down at the floor.

September 24th

MONDAY AFTERNOON, JAYLEN WAS supposed to pick-up Ebony from school, but he never showed up. She tried to call him several times on his cell phone, but it went straight to voicemail. So, like the other vehicle-less students attending Edison Tech, she boarded the bus and went home instead.

Monday evening she got a call from the Monroe County Jail. Jaylen had been arrested for possession of marijuana.

September 25th

DURING MONDAY'S SHORT PHONE
conversation with Jaylen, he had told Ebony where the
extra set of keys to his car were, and instructed her to
pick up some pick up some money from his secret
"stash" at his apartment and give the money to Loco to
bail him out of jail. Although Ebony didn't have a
license to drive, she agreed to do what he asked.

She had also found out from him how he had gotten
arrested. He was riding with a friend when the cops
pulled his friend over for a suspended tag. The friend,
an even bigger drug dealer than Jaylen, had a warrant
for his arrest for drug related charges. The police
searched the car and everyone in it. Luckily, Jaylen
only had a dime bag on him so he was not charged with

"intent to sell." His record was clean and he had no prior arrests so the public defender told him that he could post bail and would more than likely get a "slap on the wrist": one year's probation.

On Tuesday after school, Ebony took the bus to Jaylen's apartment, picked up the keys, car, and money, and took the bail money to Loco, giving him Jaylen's directions on what to do with it. As Ebony was returning back to Jaylen's place to drop the car back off, she opened his CD case to change the music, but instead of finding a good CD to listen to, she found a previously rolled blunt, ready to smoke. Temptation instantly filled her thoughts and she made a left turn at the next intersection, driving away from Jaylen's apartment and toward Irondequoit Beach.

Sitting on the rock, their rock, she lit the blunt and proceeded to smoke as if she had been doing it her whole life, not just two weeks. Everything seemed to be falling apart and she just couldn't seem to pull it all back together. She had lost her best friend, her grades in school were slipping, her little sister was mad at her, and even Momma Dee seemed displeased! She could only imagine what the members of ABLE were saying about her. She was sure that Fawn had told everyone how "stupid" she was being. *Yeah, maybe smoking weed, driving without a license, and skipping school were not the best choices, but I am having fun and I love being with Jaylen*, she rationalized. *I just wanted a little peace; what's so wrong with that?*

As she sat and puffed on joint it began to occur to her that for some reason her "high" wasn't as calming as it had been in the past. Her mind raced, clouding her brain with the worries of her drama-filled life. Her vision started to become blurry, hazy, almost distorted. Animals that were not there—could not be there—danced before her in a circle, laughing and taunting her. Unicorns, Smurfs, Care Bears, and ponies marched in sync to soundless music, some even stood atop of the water as if it were concrete.

"What's wrong with me? Am I losing my mind?" she asked herself out loud, afraid of the visual delusions surrounding her. She looked down at what was left of the joint, more than half already consumed by her. Fear gripped her as she realized that the weed must have been laced with another drug. Instantly, she threw the drug as far as she could into the lake, hoping her discarding it would take away the psychotic high, but it didn't.

For the next four hours, she sat on the rock motionless, afraid of what might happen if she moved. Slowly the drug began to wear off as the sun disappeared beyond the horizon. When the moon began to glow, the images left her and the chaotic thoughts slowed. And finally when her rumination ended, only one question remained: *Is this what I really want?*

September 26th

THE LAST ABLE MEETING of the month was held
at the Eastman Theater where the talent show would
take place only three days later. It was at this meeting
where the members were given their assignments for
the night of the talent show based on both what they
were willing to do and what special skills they each
possessed. Most of the members were assigned tasks
such as being an usher, working the vending stations, or
at the ticket booth. Along with others, Martel and
Rashan were selling hot dogs, burgers, chips, and pop,
Victor and Fawn were selling tickets, and Tamia and
Latoya were passing out programs and directing people
to their seats. A few members, including Trenton and
Ledell, helped with lighting, sound, and other technical

aspects of the program. Alisa and Omar, being the president and vice president respectively, were given the jobs of managing the talent and making sure all affairs back stage were in order. Desiree and Ebony were selected to host the show, announcing each act as it was their turn to perform on stage.

Ebony was present and on time to the ABLE meeting. Although she was a little uncertain about being a host, Mr. Armstrong assured her that she was the perfect candidate for the job. With his stamp of approval, Ebony swallowed her nerves and took on the role alongside Desiree who was a natural star.

An hour into the dry run or "dress rehearsal," Ms. Washington took the opportunity to have a one on one chat with Ebony. Ebony was sitting in the third row of the theater, watching the commotion on stage and waiting for her cue to return to the stage. Ms. Washington, noticing that she was alone, went over and sat down next to her.

"So how's it going, Ebony?" she asked in order to "break the ice."

"Okay, I guess," Ebony replied softly.

Ms. Washington smiled. "Are you ready for Saturday? Do you think you got the hang of the whole host thing?"

"Yeah. It's a little scary, but I will be alright," Ebony said, giggling a bit.

Ms. Washington's smile faded as she turned toward Ebony and softly pulled loose strand of hair away from Ebony's face. "Listen, Ebony. I've talked to Fawn and I know that you two are having a disagreement right now. I just want you to know that I am here for you and if you ever want to talk about anything, and I do mean anything, please don't hesitate to call me."

Ebony looked worriedly at Ms. Washington. "I know she told you about my boyfriend, didn't she?"

Ms. Washington sighed. "Yes, yes she did. But I am not going to judge you about him. You have to decide for yourself whether or not he is a good person for you to associate yourself with. You are a very bright, young woman. I am sure that in time, you will do what is best for Ebony."

Ebony smiled graciously. "Thanks Ms. Washington for being so understanding. I really haven't had anyone to talk to about the whole thing."

"Do you want to talk about it now?"

Ebony looked around to make sure no one else was nearby listening. "I . . . I don't know, well, maybe. I really like this guy. He makes me feel so comfortable, like I can be honest about what I am feeling. Sometimes I get so tired of everything going on in my life I just want to get away from it all. That's what I have with him, a place to escape, to get away from everything that is stressing me out." Ebony thought for a second then continued, "Maybe he's not the most perfect guy, but when we're together, it's like my problems don't exist anymore. Does that make sense?"

Ms. Washington looked at Ebony sympathetically. "Yeah, it makes perfect sense. Ebony, everyone wants to escape at certain times in their lives. That's why people go on vacations, just to get away from the issues of everyday life. But eventually, people have to come back home and face their lives again. You can't live in a fantasy because that is not life and that is not living. If you spend your entire time trying to escape from life, you will miss all the wonderful things and people that are here, in your real world. Your whole life will pass you by and you will have never had the chance to enjoy it for what it really is: hard and unpredictable, but rewarding and beautiful."

Ebony made eye contact with Ms. Washington and said meekly, "I guess I never thought about it like that."

"Yeah." Ms. Washington caringly squeezed Ebony's hand. "I need to get back to the stage, but think on that some more and let me know what you come up with."

Ebony smiled faintly and nodded. "Okay. Thanks, Ms. Washington. I'll do that."

September 27th

ON THURSDAY, EBONY SAT alone in the cafeteria during lunch, picking over her food. Ms. Washington's advice had been ringing in her ears ever since the ABLE meeting. *Am I trying to avoid life and live in a fantasy world? Am I missing out on the things I love about my real life by trying to escape?* Questions flooded her mind, most which she could not answer. Out of all of the various thoughts and questions that plagued her, the one that stood out the most was the most simplistic and complex of them all: *What do I really want?*

As if reading her mind, Fawn approached her table and sat down across from her. "You seem like you've got a lot on your mind."

Ebony looked up at her friend, someone she had known practically her whole life. This was someone who had always stood by her side and only wanted the best for her. *Why have I treated her so badly?* she thought, but the truth cut deep like a knife. The truth was that Fawn was like a mirror for her, constantly reflecting the reality of her life. Fawn represented all that she was trying to run away from, the responsibility of being Ebony. Although life in some ways was unfair, life had also brought her many gifts. Ebony would have to learn to appreciate these gifts while navigating her way through the stuff that didn't make sense or seemed too difficult to handle. Avoiding life was not the answer; alternatively, embracing it was really what needed to be done.

Ebony smiled authentically at Fawn and replied, "Yeah, I am. Fawn, I am so sorry that I've been acting so rudely to you. I really don't want to lose your friendship. You know that you are my girl and I love you to death. I was just going through a lot and was feeling sorry for myself and then Jaylen came around and I thought that . . . I don't know what I thought, but whatever it was, I was so wrong."

Fawn laughed. "I am so happy to hear you say that! I missed you so much! It was so hard watching you go through all those changes and I couldn't do anything about it. Look, I know I am a bit of a control freak, and I'm willing to work on that, but I also know that I care about you too much to just let you mess up your life, especially over a dude."

Ebony reached across the table and grabbed Fawn's hand. "I know you do and that's why you're my best friend; because you will be honest with me no matter what. Thanks for not giving up on me."

Fawn blinked back a few tears that were threatening to spill out from the corners of her eyes. "I would never give up on you." Fawn smiled and released Ebony's hand, unsure of how to ask her the next question troubling her mind. "So, are you still going out with Jaylen?"

Ebony sighed heavily, knowing that was the million dollar question. "Actually he's in jail. It's a long story, but I think he should be getting out any day now; he's just waiting for his bail to be set."

Fawn's jaw dropped in surprise. "Are you serious?"

"Yeah, but when he gets out I am thinking about ending it. I mean he's a decent guy; he's not as bad as you think. But being with him means losing the people and things in my life that are important and I just can't risk that." A tear fell swiftly down Ebony's cheek which she immediately wiped away.

"I'm sorry if I made you feel like you had to choose," Fawn replied humbly.

Ebony shook her head slowly. "It's not your fault. His lifestyle is just opposite of the lifestyle that I want for myself. I don't want to be bailing my man out of jail and hanging on the streets all the time. I want to go to college, have a professional career, wear bangin' suits to work every day, that type of stuff!" She stopped talking to laugh, then continued, "I like helping people and doing good deeds and feeling like my mom would be proud of me. I can't have that with Jaylen; he doesn't understand that kind of life."

Fawn could sense the intense pain that her friend was feeling. "Are you going to be okay?" she asked, but already knew Ebony's wasn't.

"Honestly, I'm not sure. But one day at a time, right?" Ebony glanced up feeling somewhat optimistic.

Fawn bit her lip and nodded in response. "Right."

September 28th

ON FRIDAY, JAYLEN MADE BAIL. He sent her a text message as soon as he had gotten out that he would pick her up from school. She was in sixth period, Social Studies, when her cell phone vibrated in her book bag alerting her of the new message. As she read his text, she sighed, considering what needed to be done. With the courage that she could muster up, she sent him a text back: NO. DON'T PICK ME UP. GOT A RIDE. MEET ME @ MY HOUSE @ 5.

As 5 o'clock approached, Ebony paced back and forth on the wooden porch of her grandmother's house. She had never broken up with someone and was unsure of how it would all turn out. *He's going to hate me*, she told herself. *I don't think I can do this!*

Time ran out when his Honda Civic pulled up to the curb in front of her house. He saw her standing on the porch and beeped his horn to get her to come over to him. *He thinks I am going with him*, she said under her breath. *OMG! This is going to be real interesting!*

She cautiously approached the vehicle, but on the driver side versus the passenger side as he expected. As she made her way to the door, he rolled down the window to talk to her, unsure of what she was up to.

He leaned out the window and grabbed her hand, kissing her knuckles while all the while smiling confidently. "Hey, you! I missed you so much."

"Hey, Jaylen," she replied unenthusiastically.

He pressed the lock button on the driver side, unlocking all of the car doors. "Come on, get in. I need to make a run real quick, but then we can hang out, just you and me."

Ebony pulled her hand out of his grasp and stepped away from the curb. "I . . . I can't go with you."

The confident smile faded from Jaylen's face. "Oh. You got other plans?"

"Not exactly," Ebony said.

Jaylen noticed her defensive stance and asked, "What's going on baby girl? Why you actin' strange?"

Ebony rubbed the back of her neck and exhaled loudly. "Jaylen, I'm going to be honest with you. I've really enjoyed being your girl, it's been fun. But I don't think we can do this anymore."

Jaylen's demeanor turned serious and slightly distraught. "Why? Is there somebody else? What's going on, Ebony."

"No, there's nobody else. It's not like that. Ever since I hooked up with you, I've been messing up. My grades are slipping, everyone is mad at me, I'm doing stuff that I know I should not be doing. I can't be with you because being with you means giving up what's important to me. I'm not like you, Jaylen. I want more than just the streets. I have a chance to make it in this world and I want to take it. If I fail in school or get high all the time, I'm going to ruin my future. I can't do that. I'm sorry." She searched his face for an indication that he understood her. She found none.

He chucked in disbelief. "So you're just going to leave like that?"

"Unfortunately, I have to."

"We can work this out, Ebony."

"I . . . I don't think so. I got to go." Ebony turned quickly and walked back toward the house, forcing herself to do so without looking back.

Jaylen couldn't belief his eyes or his ears. She would turn around and come back, she had to. "Ebony! Ebony! Come on girl! Ebony!" he called out, but did not get the response he desired. She went into the house and closed the door. After three minutes of waiting for her to return and several unanswered calls to her cell phone, he gave up and drove away from her house.

September 29th

PROJECT: WISE UP WAS a major success. Over five hundred people showed up for the talent show/AIDS benefit. With ticket sales and vending revenues, over $5,000 was raised for local families struggling with AIDS. The members of ABLE were so excited to see what their efforts had produced: hope.

The show began with Mr. Armstrong and Ms. Washington taking the stage and welcoming the crowd to the event, as well as introducing Desiree and Ebony as the evening's hosts.

Ebony appeared on stage wearing a long, red, satin gown with spaghetti straps and matching red, 2-inch pumps. Her hair was neatly twisted into a bun which rested at the top of her head. Her ears and neck were adorned in imitation rubies that sparkled under the spotlight like the real thing.

"Tonight you will witness the talent of fifteen amazing performances by local teenagers. They will sing for you, dance, act, and even tell you a few jokes. But although you will be entertained by the close of this evening, our hope is that you will also leave educated and informed. AIDS is a deadly and rapidly growing disease caused by Human Immunodeficiency Virus, better known as HIV. There are a lot of myths out there about this medical condition and tonight we intend to set the record straight. The only way to protect yourself and your loved ones is to empower yourself with knowledge. This evening we give you the gift of knowledge." Energetic applause followed Ebony's last sentence. She smiled graciously and passed the microphone to Desiree who looked just a fabulous wearing red dress pants, a red blazer, and a black camisole with black heels and similar ruby jewelry.

"Our first act of the evening is sure to start the night off with a bang. She is a senior at East High School planning to attend college next year and major in education. He is a junior at Wilson High and the student director of Wilson's Gospel Choir. Ladies and Gentlemen, prepare your ears for the sultry sounds of Miss Crystal Parker singing the Black National Anthem, followed by the powerful sound of Mr. Jonathan Hill singing the U.S. National Anthem."

The curtain opened and a young man and woman were spotted in the center of the stage. The young woman stepped forward to the microphone which was cradled into its stand. Moments later, the music began and so did she. "Lift every voice and sing . . ."

After several minutes of the amazing voice, the music changed and the young man replaced her at the microphone. His voice was also magnificent, and a few minutes later he ended strong with, ". . . And the home of the braveeeee!"

The remainder of the night continued in the same fashion. Ebony would provide a fact or dispel a myth about HIV/AIDS and Desiree would announce the next act. Each performance was well organized and completed with passion and precision. The program lasted three hours with the final act of the night being an interpretive dance about a loved one dying because of AIDS, set to the song "I Will Always Love You." When the music ended, there was not a dry eye in the theater.

For the last time, Ebony took the stage, but this time, all of the members of ABLE joined her. With sadness in her voice she began her final speech. "AIDS and HIV are very real issues in this world. Those of us who have not been affected by these diseases think that we are not susceptible to its destruction. I was one of those people until three years ago when my mother told me that she had been diagnosed with full-blown AIDS. She died less than two years later. She was a good woman and a good mother; her two children still need her. This disease has no prejudices or preferences. All of us are at risk so we must wise up. We must avoid unsafe sex and unsanitary needles. We have to take ownership of our lives and teach those around us what we know and have learned. I would like to personally dedicate this evening to the memory of my mother, Regina Pearson, as well as the memory of every single person who has been a victim of this illness. We will always love you."

Author's Note

THE READY & ABLE TEEN FICTION SERIES
was an idea that was birthed in 2006 during my
experience working as a mental health counselor with
troubled children. I wanted to promote reading amongst
my clients; however, I found that there were limited
books written for and about African American youth
that was actually age appropriate and void of material
that I, as a mentor, would consider offensive. In
response to this deficiency, my journey to creating
stories for this critical population began.

The most difficult aspect of writing for urban,
African American teenagers is developing stories that
are relatable to their experiences yet tastefully written.
These particular young adults are exposed to the harsh
realities of our world and many times find themselves

thrust into adult situations, having to make adult decisions. Despite their adult-like appearance and attitude, they are still adolescents and still require guidance and direction. In addition, they are not mentally prepared to handle many adult themes and concepts, and therefore, should not be inappropriately exposed to them.

The Ready & ABLE series attempts to bring to the forefront common issues that influence urban, teenage life in an authentic yet optimistic manner. Real life concerns such as drug use, racism, poverty, gangs, and romantic relationships are explored with sensitivity to both parental objections and teenage vulnerability. It is my hope that parents and teens will be able to read these stories together and have open and honest conversations about the matters that influence teen life. It is also my expectation that young adults reading these books will not only relate to the characters and scenarios presented, but also learn to be better decision makers and leaders in their communities.

Happy Reading!
A'ndrea J. Wilson, PhD

About the Author

DR. A'NDREA J. WILSON is the author of seven titles and the co-author of two projects. Her Young Adult series, Ready & ABLE Teens was introduced in 2010 and has been steadily gaining attention in schools and in the literary community. She is available for workshops and seminars and can be reached for booking at drajwilson@gmail.com or visit her website at www.andreawilsononline.com.

Book Club/Reading Group Questions

Relationships

1. Ebony is 16 years old when she starts dating Jaylen. This is her first romantic relationship. At what age do you think it is appropriate to start dating? Why?

2. Although Jaylen appears to be a nice guy, he is also involved with illegal activities which eventually lead to his arrest. Do you think Ebony did the right thing by giving Jaylen a chance to date her despite knowing he was involved with drugs? Why or why not?

3. Ebony and Fawn stopped being friends because Fawn disapproved of Jaylen. Do you think that Fawn did the right thing by insisting that Ebony stay away from Jaylen? Why or why not? Have you ever had a fight with a friend related to someone they were dating? What happened?

AIDS/HIV

4. Ebony's mother died from a battle with AIDS which is caused by HIV. How do people contract HIV? How can teens protect themselves from getting HIV?

5. Do you know anyone with HIV/AIDS or who has died from complications related to the disease? How should you treat someone who is infected with HIV or AIDS?

Drugs/Marijuana

6. Many people view marijuana as harmless and not a "real" drug; however, it is illegal in the US and does have harmful effects. What are the gangers of marijuana use?

7. Do you or teens you know smoke "weed" or use other drugs? How can the use of drugs prevent the achievement of goals and dreams?

8. On September 25th, Ebony smokes marijuana that is laced with another drug, causing her to become delusional. How dangerous is this and why?

Choices

9. What good choices did Ebony make during the course of this book? What rewards did Ebony experience as a result of her good choices?

10. What bad choices did Ebony make during the course of this book? What consequences did Ebony experience as a result of her bad choices?

Leadership

11. ABLE is all about teens demonstrating leadership in their homes, schools, and communities. Leaders take initiative (begin without having to be told to start), exhibit integrity (do the right thing/honesty), express selflessness (put others before themselves), and exceed standards (do more than what is necessary or expected). List the actions of Ebony and her friends that you believe are demonstrations of leadership. What things can you do to demonstrate leadership in your home, school, and community?

Ready & ABLE Teens Series

Volume 1 – Ebony's Bad Habit

Volume 2 – Desiree Dishes the Dirt

Volume 3 – Victor Rocks the Vote*

(*Available November 2012)

17822752R00084